Aladdin

Plurus

A STORY FROM
The Thousand and One Nights

ILLUSTRATIONS BY
Francesca Rossi

TEXT ADAPTATION GIADA FRANCIA

GRAPHIC DESIGN MARINELLA DEBERNARDI

In a remote city in Arabia, the name of which escapes me, there lived a woman and her son, Aladdin. The woman, who had been a widow for many years, was a dressmaker, but her work brought in barely enough money to keep the two of them.

As soon as Aladdin was old enough to learn a trade, his mother took him to her workshop and tried to show him how to use a needle. But Aladdin was a rebellious young man, stubborn and disobedient. Whether she was gentle with him or threatened to punish him, he refused to learn. Instead, Aladdin would run off and wander aimlessly through the narrow city streets. Sometimes he did not return home until evening. He passed entire days in this way, his only companion being his pet monkey, Abu, who went with him everywhere.

One day, while wandering in the bazaar with Abu, Aladdin accidentally bumped into a stranger, causing the man to fall over. He did not notice that the man's anger turned to delight as soon as he saw Aladdin.

Aladdin was a rebellious young man who loved to wander the streets of the city.

The man was, in fact, a magician. He had arrived in the city just two days before with the sole purpose of finding the boy whose face he kept seeing in his crystal ball. He did no know the boy's name or his age, but now he had found him. The boy was Aladdin! The magician knew that only Aladdin was able to help him.

"Are you hurt?" asked Aladdin, as he helped the man to his feet.

"Not at all," replied the magician. "You are very thoughtful! You remind me of your father when he was young. You look so like him, too!"

"You knew my father?" Aladdin asked, astonished.

"Of course," the magician lied. "I was one of his dearest friends! Come, let us have lunch and we can talk." And the two of them went into a nearby tavern.

"I'm so glad to have met you," the magician said some time later. "I have been away travelling for many years and I never expected to meet the son of my old friend when I returned home! Now I know you, I feel closer to your father. I hope you will think of me as a dear uncle."

"Yes, gladly," replied Aladdin.

Aladdin had never been in such a stylish tavern before, and had never eaten such good food! Abu, his monkey, seemed to enjoy it as much as he did! He decided he was very lucky to have met this old friend of his father.

"I imagine that you, Aladdin, have taken up your father's work?" the magician asked him.

"No . . . I . . . That is, not yet . . ."

"But, my dear boy, you certainly cannot spend every day walking the streets! I can show you how you can become rich like me."

"Yes, please do!" Aladdin replied.

"Well, let us waste no more time. You must come with me to the Mountain of Spirits."

"But that is far, far away, beyond the desert! Why do we have to go there?" Aladdin asked.

"If you do as I say, you will become richer than you ever imagined. We will leave tomorrow, at dawn."

The following morning, Aladdin met the magician as planned. They travelled all day, taking it in turns to ride on the magician's camel. It was exhausting, but the magician kept Aladdin entertained with many amusing stories about his travels.

Finally, they saw the Mountain of Spirits on the horizon, and many hours later, they arrived at the foot of the mountain.

"Let us stop here," the magician said to Aladdin. "I want you to see some amazing things that few people have ever seen. Now, go and collect the driest twigs that you can find and we can light a fire."

It wasn't long before Aladdin had collected more than enough. He returned to find the magician seated on the ground, staring intently into his crystal ball.

"You're a magician!" cried Aladdin in astonishment.

"One of the most powerful, my dear boy, but despite this I cannot enter the cave," the magician replied, lighting the pile of twigs. "It has been revealed to me that only one man in a thousand years is able to enter the cave. That man is you, Aladdin. You must enter the cave for me."

They carried on through the desert for many hours until the Mountain of Spirits appeared on the horizon.

"But what are you talking about?" replied Aladdin. "There is no cave here!"

The magician pulled a bunch of herbs out of his bag and threw it into the flames.

"Now you'll see!" he said.

A cloud of very dense smoke rose up, and the magician wafted it from side to side, uttering words that Aladdin did not understand. Suddenly the earth shook and burst open at their feet, revealing the narrow entrance to an underground cave.

Aladdin was scared and tried to escape, but the magician held him back. "There is treasure in this cave that will make you richer than the greatest sultan on Earth. But first you must do exactly what I tell you," said the magician. "Listen carefully. When you go into the cave, you will find three large rooms. You will need to pass through all of them. In each one you will see on either side four bronze urns filled with gold and silver. You must not touch them! If you do you will die instantly. Beyond the third room, you will find a garden full of trees, all laden with fruit.

Aladdin was scared and tried to escape, but the magician held him back.

You can take as much of this fruit as you want, but you must be quick. Next, go up the staircase with fifty steps, which will take you to a terrace. There you will see before you a lighted lamp stand in the hollow of a rock. Take it, extinguish the flame, and bring it to me. Now go, my boy," he said. "And remember, if you do as I say, we'll both be rich for the rest of our lives."

With one effortless leap, Aladdin entered the cave. He passed through each of the rooms that the magician had mentioned, taking care not to touch the large urns. When he came to the garden he stopped, awestruck by the wonderful sight ahead of him . . .

The trees were laden with colourful fruits, but he could see that they were no ordinary fruits. The white fruits were actually glittering pearls, the transparent ones were sparkling diamonds, the dark red ones were rubies, the green ones were emeralds . . . All were of a size and perfection that Aladdin had never before seen. He did not believe there were any more beautiful, anywhere in the world.

Aladdin seized handfuls of the jewels and filled his pockets. When he could no longer fit any more in, he put them in the folds of his belt and inside his shirt.

Weighed down with so much wealth, he climbed the staircase, took the old lamp the magician had described to him, and blew out the flame. Then he quickly retraced his steps until he reached the entrance to the cave.

The magician was waiting impatiently.

As soon as Aladdin saw him, he said, "Please, give me your hand and help me up."

"Give me the lamp first, it will only hinder you," the magician replied. But there was something in the way the magician said this that meant Aladdin did not quite trust him.

"I'll give it to you as soon as I'm out of here," said Aladdin.

Aladdin had indeed been right to mistrust the magician, who had planned to take the lamp, but leave Aladdin where he was. The magician was furious and tried in vain to cast a spell to get the lamp. Finally he gave up. He threw some herbs on the fire, uttered two magic words, and a great rock rolled across the cave entrance, sealing it.

Aladdin began to shout and beat his fists against the rock but he soon realised that he could not move it. He sat down to try to think what he could do in this terrible situation. He thought perhaps there was another entrance, but how could he find it? The cave was now very dark.

Suddenly Aladdin remembered the old lamp. He pulled it out of his pocket and rubbed it to try to light it. What happened next took his breath away!

A spiral of blue smoke began to rise out of the lamp, slowly at first, then faster and faster, until it filled every corner of the cave.

Aladdin dropped the lamp, which began to turn around by itself, then, propelled by an invisible force, it rose into the air.

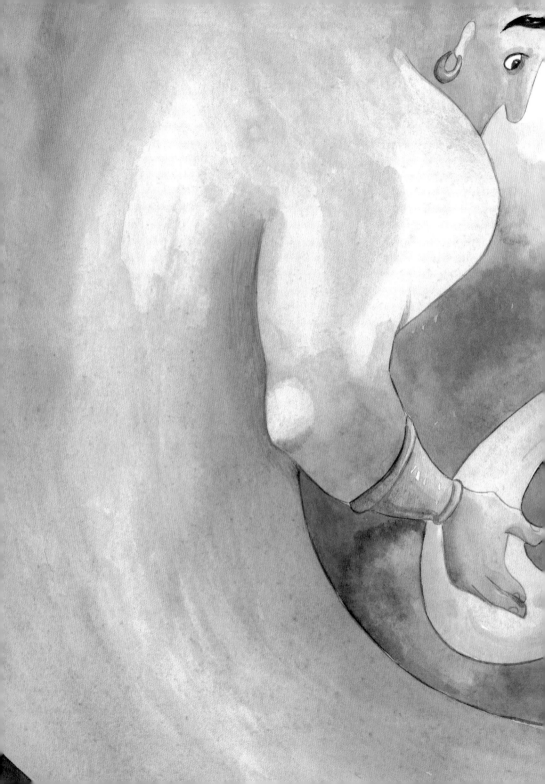

At that moment, a dazzling blue light illuminated the cave, forcing Aladdin to cover his face with his hands. When he lowered them, he saw before him, hovering in midair, a huge, glowing genie.

"You have freed me from the lamp that has been my prison for thousands of years," said the genie to Aladdin, bowing. "I am grateful, my master. Your wish is my command."

Aladdin thought he was dreaming. He said the first thing that came into his head. "Take me back home at once."

No sooner had he uttered these words than the earth burst open and he found himself standing outside the cave. The genie held Aladdin in his arms, and flew back along the route that he and the magician had taken just that morning.

Soon Aladdin found himself back at his house. He called loudly for his mother to come and see the lamp and the precious stones he had collected in the cave.

Aladdin explained what had happened. "Our troubles are over!" he declared. "First, we will get a new shop for you. It will be much more elegant, and brighter and bigger! You can stop doing small repairs and use your talents to make clothes for wealthy ladies. What do you say?" he asked, hugging her.

"It is wonderful indeed, Aladdin!" said his mother. "But there is one thing I want to know. Now that you are so rich, how will you spend your time?"

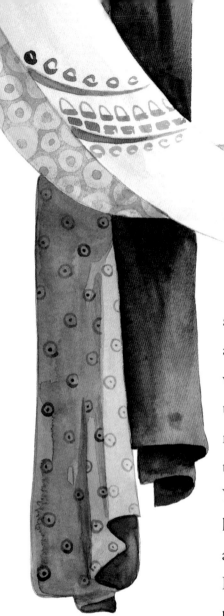

"It's strange," said Aladdin, as he stroked Abu. "Now that I'm rich and I could spend all day in bed if I wanted, I feel I must do something useful. I want to have a business of my own, that will be successful. I think I will become a cloth merchant. You and I can work together," he told his mother. "I'll bring you the cloth, and you can sew it. Never again will I go wandering around the streets, I promise." And with that, he hugged his stunned mother.

"And now, let's celebrate!" Aladdin said as he rubbed the lamp.

When the genie appeared Aladdin said, "Please could you arrange a banquet for me and my mother?"

Instantly, a large silver tray appeared on the genie's head. On the tray were twelve gold dishes filled with delicious food, six large loaves of bread as white as snow, and two bottles of excellent wine. The genie put everything on the table and then disappeared.

From that day, Aladdin worked hard and, with the help of the genie, he became known as an honest merchant who imported rare and precious fabrics from distant lands.

One morning, while Aladdin was working in the bazaar, the sultan's guards appeared and ordered everyone to go indoors. The royal carriage carrying Princess Jasmine, was passing through on its way to the palace. No one was allowed to see the princess.

But Princess Jasmine herself longed to visit the bazaar. She decided that today at least would be different. She stopped the carriage and slipped out before her father's guards could stop her.

Usually Princess Jasmine spent the whole day alone. She knew that soon she would be shut up inside the walls of the palace again and she wanted to see as much as she could now. When she passed a fortune teller's shop, she decided it would be fun to have her fortune told, and she slipped inside.

It was here that Aladdin first saw her. He had taken refuge in the fortune teller's shop. He stayed, hidden behind a curtain, watching Jasmine.

Her face was hidden behind a veil and he longed to see it. And as if he had said the words aloud, little Abu took a great leap, landed on the princess's shoulder, and lifted her veil for a moment. Aladdin was dazzled by Jasmine's beauty and fell in love instantly.

That evening, at home with his mother, Aladdin was quiet and thoughtful. He sighed all the way through dinner. She was surprised to see him so sad and dreamy. It was very unlike him!

She asked if something had happened or if perhaps he was feeling ill.

She listened very carefully as her son started to tell her what had happened. Then Aladdin told her that he was going to ask for the princess's hand in marriage.

At that point, she could not help but interrupt him with a loud laugh. "Oh, my son! You must have lost your mind to speak in such a way."

But seeing that he was serious, she agreed to take a gift to the sultan – the precious stones that Aladdin had found in the cave.

In the light of the sun, the gems were breathtaking. The

variety of colour, and the way they sparkled dazzled [*unpressed*] both mother and son. Aladdin hoped that the sultan would be impressed by them and he would be allowed to meet him.

Aladdin's mother took the pot of precious stones and made her way to the sultan's palace. She was shown into a beautiful room, long and spacious. The sultan sat there, his advisors [*who gives advice*] on either side of him.

Trembling, she offered the gift to the sultan and asked if her would meet her son. The sultan and his advisors were so intrigued [*curious*] by the jewels that they agreed.

"He will receive you, Aladdin!" she told him as soon as she got home.

"But when can I go to him? When can I ask for Jasmine's hand in marriage?" Aladdin asked.

"In exactly one month!", said his mother, expecting him to be pleased.

"A month? That's too long for me to wait!" said Aladdin. Upset, he took the lamp and summoned [*called*] the genie.

"What is your desire? [*wish*]" the genie asked when he appeared.

"Genie, grant me a wish. I want to talk to Princess Jasmine."

Aladdin explained to him that he must see the princess. He had to talk to her, and show her he loved her.

The genie nodded. He waved of his hand and a carpet appeared before them.

Aladdin sat on the carpet and immediately it lifted off the floor and began circling the room before flying out of the window. Aladdin found that he was able to guide the carpet with his thoughts, and he directed it to the sultan's palace. It was in darkness, except for one room at the top of a high tower – it was Princess Jasmine's room!

Jasmine had not able to get to sleep that night. She was furious! During dinner, yet another suitor had been presented to her. He was one of the richest and most noble men in the East, but she thought he was foolish and she refused to marry him.

"You must choose a husband!" said her father. "It will soon be your birthday and then, according to the law, you must marry."

Jasmine was now pacing back and forth in her room, thinking. She wanted to be married, but only for love,

and more than anything else she wanted to get out of the palace and be free!

At that moment, she heard a noise outside the window. She leant out and was astonished to see a young man who seemed to be floating in the air on a carept!

"Your Highness, I would like to explain that —"

"Take me away!" Jasmine said at once. "Let me ride on your carpet! Help me get out of the palace!"

Aladdin could not believe what he was hearing. Without saying a word, he steered the carpet closer to the window to allow Jasmine to get onto it and then they flew away.

They flew over the city in silence, but then Aladdin steered the magic carpet to the summit of a mountain, where it stopped. They looked at one another. Then, as they both started to talk at the same time, they laughed.

Jasmine immediately fell in love with this young man who had dared to take her away from the palace.

Dawn came all too soon, and they returned. But as they flew to the tower, they saw that there was a great commotion in the courtyard. Jasmine's disappearance had

been discovered and the sultan was ordering the guards to start a search.

The princess ran to him and then she introduced Aladdin to her father.

"Your Magnificence," Aladdin said, unable to stop himself. "I love your daughter. Please let me marry her."

But the sultan was furious. "How dare you?" he said. "You are not worthy of my daughter!"

"Father, you said that I must marry before my birthday! I choose Aladdin," the princess said.

The sultan knew how stubborn Jasmine could be and that he would not be able to change her mind. But he could not allow her to marry this man. Then he had an idea – he would set Aladdin an impossible task.

"I will allow you to marry my daughter," he said to Aladdin. "But only if you are able to build a palace in three days. It must be made entirely of gold and precious stones. If you fail, you will die."

Jasmine was very upset, but Aladdin smiled as he ran home to rub his lamp!

The sultan
was furious.
The princess
had run away
and must
be found.

"What is your ~~command~~ order, young master?" said the genie, emerging from the ~~lamp~~. Come out / appear

"You must help me win Princess Jasmine's hand by building the largest palace the city has ever seen. You have three days," said Aladdin. "If you can do that, you will make me the happiest man alive!"

"Three days?" said the genie. "I only need three hours!" So saying, the genie took Aladdin to a rooftop from which he could follow the work. With sudden flashes of light, the genie created the walls of a sumptuous grand / huge palace and carved them with ornaments and decorations.

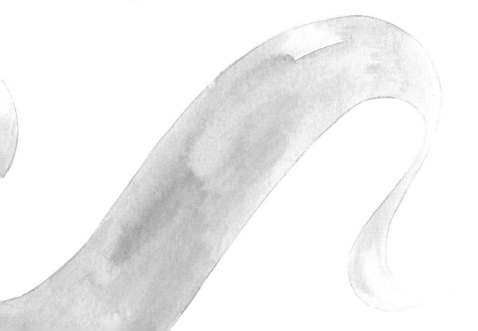

Just over two hours later, the genie came back to Aladdin, and said, "My young master, your palace is finished. Come and see if my work is satisfactory!" And he took Aladdin to the palace.

to meet expectations

Aladdin walked through the halls of the palace breathless with wonder. Everywhere he found wealth, elegance and magnificence. It was truly worthy of the princess!

deserves

Everyone was astounded to see the beautiful palace. The news of this incredible wonder spread quickly and the sultan had no choice but to agree to the marriage.

difficult to believe

Aladdin and Jasmine married just a week later. The wedding banquet took place at the new palace, and even the sultan was impressed. The festivities lasted for days, and there was much music and dancing. Aladdin truly was the happiest man alive!

party

celebration

Meanwhile, the evil magician who had shut Aladdin in the cave all those months ago had not forgotten him. He was certain that Aladdin must have perished, but he now decided to find out for sure what had become of him.

died

He took his crystal ball out and gazed [stare] into it . . .

When he found out that not only had Aladdin escaped from the cave, but he was now immensely [extremely] rich, and was the honoured and respected husband of a princess, he was furious. "That wretched [evil/bad] boy must have discovered the secret of the lamp!" he said to himself.

Early next morning, he set off on his camel for the distant Arabian city where Aladdin lived. He knew that he had to steal the lamp from Aladdin, but first he needed to know where it was.

As soon as he reached the city, he looked into his crystal ball. He saw that Aladdin was on a journey to buy new fabrics and at first he worried that he would surely have taken the lamp with him. But then he saw that he had left the lamp at his palace.

The magician realised he must act at once, and devise a ~~create~~ plan to get the lamp. First he went to the bazaar and bought ~~a market place~~ a range of different lamps. Then, posing as a dealer in rare ~~pretended~~ and valuable objects, he knocked at the door of Aladdin's palace.

Princess Jasmine welcomed him. As he sipped tea with the princess and discussed all his wares, he saw the lamp the ~~objects~~ he so desired standing on the table. He could not believe his luck!

"I'm surprised to see that a lady as elegant as Your Highness has such an old and shabby lamp in her home," he said. "I would be honoured to be allowed to exchange it for one that is far rarer and more beautiful!" He made it sound as if his offer was very generous.

Jasmine had no idea that the genie existed. She accepted the new lamp with delight.

But as soon as the magician had the old lamp in his hands, he rubbed it, and the genie appeared. He bowed to his new master.

"First, you will carry me and this entire palace, including the princess, far away from here. I want Aladdin to go back to being the penniless good-for-nothing that he once was!" the magician said.

The genie was furious, and tried to free himself from the lamp, but the magic that forced him to obey the lamp's owner was much stronger than his. He had to do as the magician commanded him.

Aladdin returned from his trip and soon realised what had happened. "Where shall I find my princess?" he asked himself desperately. "I have no idea where the magician has taken her, or my palace. How can I find them without the genie's help?"

For days he sat in the place where his palace had stood. Neither his mother nor the sultan could persuade him to move. Even Abu failed to make him smile.

"Abu, my little monkey, she that I hold most dear in the world, has vanished. I wish I could go back to the day I met her, to the moment I first saw her. I remember I was in the fortune teller's shop, and . . . Wait a minute!" he cried, jumping to his feet. "I have an idea! The fortune teller understands magic. If there is one person in the whole city who can help me find them it is she!"

So saying, Aladdin raced to the fortune teller's shop, his monkey clinging to his shoulder.

Aladdin had not been there for a while, and he almost missed the entrance. It was hidden behind a heavy tapestry embroidered with stars and moons.

Finally Aladdin found it. When he pulled back the tapestry a ray of sunlight shone on the face of the fortune teller.

"I've been waiting for you, Aladdin. It's been a long time since we last met. It was the same day the princess came to me to find out her future. I told her that she would meet a brash young man and fall in love, and that one day she would disappear together with the palace that he had built for her. But she didn't believe me."

"So you already know everything!" said Aladdin, amazed. "You must know what has happened to Jasmine!"

"I know that a magician has taken her away, to punish you."

"But do you know how I can find him?" Aladdin asked.

"Magic always leaves a trail," said the fortune teller. "I can follow it and show you the way."

"Please, I beg you!" Aladdin said.

As soon as the fortune teller had told him the place where the magician had taken the princess and the palace, Aladdin ran to his mother's house, to get the magic carpet.

In a few short hours, flying faster than the wind, Aladdin arrived in the middle of the desert. There his palace now stood, not far from a big city. The carpet landed right under the windows of Princess Jasmine's rooms.

Abu climbed up onto the ledge, and tapped lightly on the window to attract her attention. When Jasmine leant out and saw Aladdin she was very happy! As she opened her mouth to speak, he motioned for her to be quiet.

"Jasmine, is the magician here?" he whispered.

"Yes, he is. I have been so frightened, Aladdin. What do we do now?" she whispered back.

"I have thought of a plan. You must invite the magician to join you for tea and —"

"But I hate that man! I can't bear to look at him," she said.

"Please do as I say. While he is distracted Abu and I will try to steal the lamp," he replied.

"Don't you think you could have told me about the genie?" Jasmine said angrily. "How could you have kept him hidden from me?"

Abu grabbed the
lamp and brought
it to Aladdin
who immediately
summoned
the genie.

"Yes, you're right," Aladdin said. "I thought perhaps you wouldn't love me if you knew that he had helped me win your hand in marriage. I was wrong and I won't keep things from you any more. But tell me where the lamp is ~~go~~, and then please do as I ask!"

As soon as he saw the magician come to Jasmine, Aladdin entered the palace through the kitchen door. He crossed the courtyard and began to climb the stairs to the room where the magician kept the lamp.

When he tried to open the door, however, he found it was locked. "How are we going to get in?" he said to Abu. Suddenly he had an idea. He took the monkey in his arms, went up the stairs, and came out onto a balcony that overlooked the room. Then he said to Abu, "Can you go down there and get the lamp?"

Abu wrapped his tail around the rail of the balcony and managed to stretch down and reach the lamp easily!

As soon as he had the lamp in his hands, Aladdin call
summoned the genie.

"I've missed you," the genie said. "I would appreciate it
like

if you would not allow that magician to become my master again. And what is your command, young master?"

"I would like you to take Princess Jasmine and me home. And take the magician to a place where he can never hurt us again."

"Your wish is my command!" the genie replied.

Suddenly everything was surrounded by a cloud of smoke. When the smoke cleared, they found that the palace was back in the exact spot where the genie had built it.

Then with a puff of breath, the genie created a whirlwind that lifted the magician high in the air. It took him to the other side of the world, to a small valley surrounded by towering crags, from where he would be unable to escape.

When the genie returned, Aladdin said, "I have one last wish, my friend. I wish to break the spell of the lamp. You are free to go wherever you want and do just as you please."

The genie stared at Aladdin in disbelief. Then joyfully he rose into the air and flew to the stars. For the first time in thousands of years, he enjoyed the sweet taste of freedom!

FRANCESCA ROSSI

WAS BORN IN 1983. SHE GRADUATED FROM THE
SCUOLA INTERNAZIONALE DI COMICS (INTERNATIONAL
SCHOOL OF COMICS) IN FLORENCE. SHE ILLUSTRATES
BOOKS FOR A NUMBER OF ITALIAN PUBLISHERS AND
DESIGNS BOOK COVERS AND POSTERS. ALONGSIDE HER
WORK AS AN ILLUSTRATOR, SHE CONDUCTS WORKSHOPS
IN SCHOOLS AND LIBRARIES, AS WELL AS MAKING AND
DECORATING POTTERY.

Plurus

This book is published under co-edition licence by Plurus Books,
75-76 Blackfriars Road, London SE1 8HA
www.plurusbooks.com
info@plurusbooks.com
under licence from
© 2014 De Agostini Libri S.p.A.
Via G. da Verrazano, 15 - 28100 Novara, Italy
www.whitestar.it - www.deagostini.it

Translation: Contextus s.r.l., Pavia, Italy (Louise Bostock)

ISBN 978 191027136 0
1 2 3 4 5 6   18 17 16 15 14
Printed in China